First Printing 1985

Heian International, Inc.
P.O. Box 1013
Union City, CA 94587

Originally published by Poplar Publishing Co., Tokyo

Translated by D.T. Ooka

ISBN: 0-89346-257-8

Printed in Japan

The Fisherman and the Grateful Turtle

Urashima Taro

retold by Essei Okawa

illustrated by Koichi Murakami

Heian

Long, long ago in a seaside village in Japan there lived a poor young man named Urashima Taro. He made his living by fishing and gathering clams, abalone and seaweed every day. Urashima Taro's skin was burned dark by the sun and the sea. He owned a tiny boat and lived in a simple wooden hut.

One day there was a terrible storm. As the days passed and the storm continued, the sea was so rough that Urashima Taro could not go fishing. Since he could not fish, Urashima Taro had nothing to eat. He went to bed hungry and awoke in the morning hungrier still.

When the storm finally passed and the sea was calm, Urashima Taro went out in his boat to fish. All day long he could not catch a single flounder or sea bream. By the end of the day, all he had caught were some small herring. Tired and hungry, Urashima Taro returned to shore. He secured his boat and began to walk home along the beach.

On the way home he saw some children teasing a sea turtle they had captured. "Hey there," called Urashima Taro, "Let that turtle go!" The children ignored him and began to hit and kick the turtle. "Hit it harder! Let's knock it over!" they shouted.

Urashima Taro could not ignore the children's cruelty and said, "Please let the turtle go! If you give it to me, I will give you all the fish I caught today." Reluctantly, the children gave him the turtle, took the fish, and ran home. Urashima Taro released the turtle in the ocean, saying, "That was a close call! Now hurry and go back home where you belong!" The turtle swam quickly out to sea, turning back every now and then to look at Urashima Taro as if to say, "Thank you!"

The sun had set, and the sky and ocean were a dark blue. Urashima Taro turned towards home. He was happy that he had saved the turtle, even though it meant that he would be hungry one more night. Suddenly Urashima Taro heard a soft voice calling him. "Excuse me..." When he turned around, he saw a beautiful princess hovering above the waves.

"Thank you for helping the turtle. My father, the Sea King, is very grateful and would like to thank you himself. Please come with me!" The robes of the princess fluttered as she held out her hand to Urashima Taro. A huge sea turtle swam up and motioned for Urashima Taro to climb up on its back.

"What? The Sea King wants to see me?" exclaimed Urashima Taro. He took the princess' hand and climbed up on the great turtle's back. She joined him, and the turtle began to swim out to sea. A great path through the ocean opened before them which seemed to go on forever. They skimmed over forests of kelp, passed through valleys of coral and dodged schools of fish.

As they crossed over mountains covered with starfish and clams, the shimmering Sea Palace appeared in the distance. Its pillars were made of red coral, its walls of crystal, and its roof of gold. It was truly a splendid sight! They came closer and closer until the turtle reached the front gate, which was made of amber and mother-of-pearl. The princess clapped her hands, and the gate swung open. Many servants came running out, crying, "Welcome! The Sea King has been waiting for you!"

Urashima Taro was led to a brilliantly lighted reception room where the Sea King greeted him warmly. "That turtle you rescued is one of my dearest servants," he said. "You saved him from great danger after he lost his way. As a reward, please stay here as my guest and enjoy yourself!"

The beautiful princess who had accompanied Urashima Taro reappeared wearing a crown made of pearls and a many-colored robe. She was so lovely that Urashima Taro could not stop watching her. Servants came bearing all kinds of delicacies for him to eat and drink.

“Please help yourself,” urged the Sea Princess as she poured wine and offered Urashima Taro plates of tempting food. The princess pointed towards the garden and said, “Look! The dance of the Sea Palace is about to begin!”

The sounds of music could be heard in the distance as beautiful girls began to dance. Around the girls swam fish of every color; they swam up and down, back and forth and in and out of the swirling robes. It was a wonderful sight!

The next day, the Sea Princess took Urashima Taro on a tour of the palace. He saw many wonderful things, but the most marvelous were the rooms of Spring, Summer, Autumn, and Winter. In the Spring room, Urashima Taro heard a nightengale singing on a branch of plum blossoms. Suddenly the scene changed to one of butterflies fluttering over a field of yellow flowers. Next he heard the strains of a rice-planting song, and saw the bright green rice fields. In the Summer room, he saw the twinkling stars of the Milky Way, heard a chorus of summer insects and saw flickering fireflies in the rice fields. When Urashima Taro entered the Autumn room, the scene changed to one of brilliant red maple leaves and chrysanthemums in bloom. Then he saw the rice being harvested to the sound of rice-harvesting songs. Finally, in the Winter room, he saw a peaceful white snow-covered scene. Urashima Taro could only stand in awe with his eyes wide open, uttering an occasional "Ohhhh!"

On other days Urashima Taro and the Sea Princess went on picnics and explored the mountains and valleys around the Sea Palace. Sometimes they would attend festivals and celebrations, and other times the Sea Princess would tell him wonderful stories. Urashima Taro spent his days so happily that he lost count of the time that passed.

About three years had gone by when Urashima Taro bgan to recall the seaside village where he had lived. He thought about his simple wooden hut, his tiny boat and his friends and neighbors. "I wonder how everyone is? Surely today they are out fishing." Urashima Taro sat with his chin resting in his hands, lost in thought. He no longer enjoyed eating exotic delicacies or watching beautiful girls dance. "The sea breeze always felt so good! The fish I caught with my own hands tasted the best. Even though I am poor, I want to return to my own world," he decided. Urashima Taro then told the Sea Princess of his desire.

This made the Sea Princess very sad, and she urged Urashima Taro to stay. But he remained determined to return to the world he knew. "I was meant to be a fisherman in that seaside village," he pleaded. "Please let me go home!" Reluctantly, the Sea Princess finally agreed. Then she brought him a small red box. "As a parting gift, I will give you this treasure box. Please be careful with it. It has the power to bring you back to the Sea Palace —but you must never open it!" she warned.

Urashima Taro said goodbye to the Sea King and climbed on the giant sea turtle's back, holding his treasure box under his arm. "Farewell, Urashima Taro," cried the Sea Princess, her robes fluttering as she waved. "Take care of yourself," replied Urashima Taro. As he looked back, waving goodbye, the shimmering Sea Palace disappeared in the ocean's blue depths. The giant turtle crossed the starfish and clam-covered mountains and skimmed over the forest of kelp as if it was flying over the water.

"At last! I'm home! This is my beach and my village!" thought Urashima Taro as he alighted from the turtle and ran towards the village. But what had happened? Urashima Taro's wooden hut was nowhere to be seen! The neighbors' houses all looked different, and the people living there were total strangers. "My name is Urashima Taro…I used to live in this village…" cried Urashima Taro as he wandered here and there in confusion. A very old man heard him, shook his head and said, "Urashima Taro is the name of a man from this village who saved a turtle and went to the Sea Palace. But that happened more than 300 years ago!" "What? More than 300 years ago?!" gasped Urashima Taro.

In shock, Urashima Taro ran to the shore. The sea breeze felt the same, but the young men pulling in their nets were all strangers to him. "Could it be true? I thought I was only gone for three years!" cried Urashima Taro as he knelt on the sand. Suddenly he remembered the treasure box the Sea Princess had given him. "She said the box had the power to bring me back to the Sea Palace! Surely, then, I can open it, even though she said I must not!" Urashima Taro told himself.

Slowly Urashima Taro untied the cords around the red box and lifted the lid. A thick cloud of white smoke drifted out of the box and covered him completely. When the smoke finally cleared, Urashima Taro had become a wrinkled old man with white hair!